JUV/
JONAS

NPL

W9-BWX-063

R0176033064
El trayecto = The trek

Chicago Public Library
North Pulaski Branch
4300 W. North Ave.
Chicago, IL. 60639
(312) 744-9573
Mon., Wed.10am-6pm, Fri., & Sat.:9am-5pm
Tues. & Thurs.:12pm-8pm Sunday:Closed

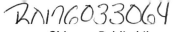
RN176033064

Chicago Public Library
North Pulaski Branch
4300 W. North Ave.
Chicago, IL. 60639
(312) 744-9573
Mon., Wed.10am-6pm, Fri., & Sat.:9am-5pm
Tues. & Thurs.:12pm-8pm Sunday:Closed

EL TRAYECTO
The Trek

Ann Jonas

Translated by Teresa Mlawer

LECTORUM
PUBLICATIONS, INC.
111 EIGHTH AVE., NEW YORK, NY 10011-5201

For Susan,
and of course,
Don, Nina & Amy

Para Susan,
y por supuesto,
Don, Nina y Amy

EL TRAYECTO
The Trek
Bilingual Edition

Copyright © 1991 by Lectorum Publications, Inc.
Originally published in English under the title
THE TREK
Copyright © 1985 by Ann Jonas

All rights reserved. No part of this book may be reproduced or utilized in any form
or by any means, electronic or mechanical, including photocopying, recording or
by any information storage and retrieval system, without permission
in writing from the Publisher.

This edition published by arrangement with the original publisher
William Morrow & Company, Inc.

Published by
Lectorum Publications, Inc.
111 Eighth Avenue
New York, NY 10011-5201

ISBN 0-9625 162-3-6

Printed in the United States of America

My mother
doesn't walk me
to school anymore.

Mi mamá
no me acompaña
más a la escuela.

But she doesn't know
we live on the edge
of a jungle.

Pero ella no sabe
que vivimos en el límite
de una selva.

She doesn't even see
what's right outside our door!

¡Ella ni siquiera ve
lo que hay junto a nuestra puerta!

There are creatures everywhere.
But they can't hide from me.

Hay animales por todas partes.
Pero no pueden esconderse de mí.

Some of my animals are dangerous
and it's only my amazing skill
that saves me day after day.

Algunos de mis animales son peligrosos
y es solamente mi extraordinaria habilidad
lo que me salva día tras día.

Look at that!
The waterhole is really
crowded today.

¡Mira eso!
El charco está muy
concurrido hoy.

What will they do when this herd
goes down to drink?

¿Qué harán ellos cuando esta manada
  baje a beber?

Here's my helper, right on time.
Now we can cross
the desert together.

Aquí está mi ayudante, justo a tiempo.
Ahora podemos cruzar
el desierto juntas.

Those animals won't see us
if we stay behind the sand dunes.
Be very quiet.

Los animales no nos verán
si nos quedamos detrás de las dunas.
¡No hagas ruido!

hat woman doesn't know
bout the animals.
she did, she'd be scared.

Esa señora no sabe nada
acerca de los animales.
Si lo supiera, se asustaría.

We missed the boat!
Now we'll have to swim
across the river.

¡Perdimos la barca!
Ahora tendremos que cruzar
el río nadando.

Be careful! This jungle is full of animals.

¡Ten cuidado! Esta selva está llena de animales.

The trading post at last!
No time to stop!

¡Al fin llegamos a la tienda rural!
¡No hay tiempo para detenerse!

We're almost there,
only the mountain
to climb.

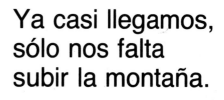

Ya casi llegamos,
sólo nos falta
subir la montaña.

We made it!   ¡Lo logramos!

SOME ANIMALS WE KNOW

ALGUNOS ANIMALES CONOCIDOS

MOOSE	ALLIGATOR	PORCUPINE	ALPACA	TURKEY	SPIDER

ALCE	CAIMÁN	PUERCO ESPÍN	ALPACA	PAVO	ARAÑA

PANGOLIN	WARTHOG	ZEBRA	MONKEY	LIZARD	BONGO

PANGOLÍN	JABALÍ VERRUGOSO	CEBRA	MONO	LAGARTO	BONGO

CAMEL	PEACOCK	YAK	VULTURE	SEA LION	LEOPARD

CAMELLO	PAVO REAL	YAC	BUITRE	LEÓN MARINO	LEOPARDO

MORE ANIMALS WE KNOW

OTROS ANIMALES QUE CONOCEMOS

OSTRICH	HIPPOPOTAMUS	KOALA	WATER BUFFALO	PIG	PYTHON

AVESTRUZ	HIPOPÓTAMO	KOALA	BÚFALO DE LA INDIA	CERDO	PITÓN

GORILLA	SWAN	RHINOCEROS	SHEEP	GIRAFFE	CASSOWARY

GORILA	CISNE	RINOCERONTE	OVEJA	JIRAFA	CASUARIO

TURTLE	ELEPHANT	TIGER	ORANGUTAN	FISH	ORYX

TORTUGA	ELEFANTE	TIGRE	ORANGUTÁN	PECES	ORIX